MENDING PETER'S HEART

MENDING PETER'S HEART

Written by Maureen Wittbold   Illustrated by Larry Salk

Published by
Portunus Publishing Co.
3435 Ocean Park Blvd., Suite 211
Santa Monica, California 90405
tel: (310) 450-5021
web site: http://www.portunus.net

Design: Egret Design
Editing: David Anderson and Andrea Tronslin

Publisher's Cataloging in Publication
(prepared by Quality Books, Inc.)

Wittbold, Maureen.
    Mending Peter's Heart/ Maureen Wittbold.
    p.cm.
    ISBN 0-9641330- 4-0
    1.Children and death--Juvenile fiction. 2. Grief--Juvenile fiction.
    I. Title.
    PZ7.W588Men 1995   [Fic]
                                  QB194-21199

Library of Congress Catalog Card Number: 98-87530

First Edition
10 9 8 7 6 5 4 3 2

This book is sincerely dedicated to my husband and children,
and written in loving memory of
Ann Harwood, Stephen Milmoe, Martha Murnane,
and Mishka.

May the hearts of their families and friends be mended.

S TOP GIVING ME ICE CREAM! I CAN'T STAND ICE CREAM!"
shouted Peter flinging his bowl across the room. Startled, Peter's
parents looked up. Peter wrenched open the door and ran out of
the house.

"Peter, get back here," scolded his father, following him. The
door banged shut with an angry slap.

Peter's mother watched her son from the window. "Let him
go," she said.

Peter hurried down the sidewalk as if pushed by a mighty and furious wind. "Mishka, Mishka, Mishka," he thought as his feet pounded the pavement. "Come back, Mishka, I love you," he cried, covering his face with his hands and sinking onto the curb.

9

A tap on his back made him look up. Peter's eyes followed the length of the cane touching his shoulder until he looked into the face of his neighbor, Mr. MacIntyre.

"Peter, my friend, you look a million miles away. What's on your mind?"

"My dog's gone."

"Gone? Gone where? Lost? Stolen?"

"Just gone," Peter answered, "as far away as you can go. She's dead, Mr. Mac. Dead. I could wish on birthday candles and shooting stars, but she's never, ever coming back."

Mr. Mac reached down. "Peter, come help an old man up to his porch. I have a rocking chair that's been needing a body in it for some time now."

"The first step is always the trickiest," said Mr. Mac, steadying himself with his cane, "so don't go rushing on up when I need you." He put his hand on Peter's shoulder and together they made their way up the stairs.

"Sit down and rock a bit. Medicine for the soul is what a rocking chair is. Go on, sit," said Mr. Mac, motioning to the chair. "This one's mine."

Peter began to rock, keeping pace with the rapid beat of his heart.

"You're moving awful fast, Peter. You got some place to go?"

Peter's hands trailed over the wood. It was as smooth and brown and warm as autumn chestnuts. His rocking grew restful.

I t's not fair, Mr. Mac. Why did Mishka have to die?"

"Sometimes there isn't a single reason in the world for something to happen. The way I figure it, Peter, you can't stop the seasons from changing or the sun from setting on a life. Didn't always think that way, though." Mr. Mac shook his head. "When it happened to me, it darn near wore me out. There was no talking sense to me then."

"I was like that today. I threw a bowl of ice cream."

"Ice cream? Why ice cream? I thought all you young'uns loved ice cream."

"Not when they give it to you a hundred times a day," grumbled Peter.

"Comfort food, I call it," said Mr. Mac. "Hot chocolate in the winter, ice cream in the summer."

"Well, I can't stand ice cream," hissed Peter through clenched teeth.

"Just calm yourself down now, Peter. I reckon there's not much you do like these days. Can't say that I blame you, though." Mr. Mac studied Peter's face. "Now, go on, tell me about this friend of yours."

S he was the most beautiful Husky there ever was. Now, she's gone."

"I lost someone beautiful, too, Peter." Mr. Mac's eyes narrowed and dimmed, like candles startled by a sudden wind.

"She was my best friend," Peter said. Mr. Mac nodded his head in understanding.

A long time ago—when I was a baby, that is—I used to hold onto her ears and drink my bottle. My mom called Mishka my 'doggie blanket.'"

"Imagine that," Mr. Mac laughed. His laughter tugged Peter's mouth into a small smile.

"I could take two days to tie my shoes, and she'd still wait for me."

A patient friend. They're real hard to find. I'll bet you could look into her eyes and know she loved you."

"Hey, Mr. Mac, how did you know that?"

"I've seen that look, Peter. It goes right down to your heart and kind of lights you up like a jack-o'-lantern."

She got really sick, though. So sick, Mr. Mac, I had to help her do almost everything. She couldn't even walk. If I was strong enough I would have carried her."

"I did,"murmured Mr. Mac, remembering.

"I had to feed her," said Peter.

"Same as you'd feed a baby," said Mr. Mac as a tear silently slipped down his cheek.

"She couldn't see." Peter closed his own eyes.

"We had to help them find their way," said Mr. Mac, looking off in the distance to the gentle hills.

"I put my arms around her. I said, I love you, Mishka, please don't leave. She felt so warm. I didn't want to let go. Then, I kissed her and said good-bye."

"Good-byes are something awful, Peter, but at least we got to do that. Not everyone gets the chance to say farewell to a friend."

Sometimes I think she's next to me," said Peter, putting his hand out, "and I reach for her at night."

"So do I," whispered Mr. Mac. Their hands touched as softly as the wings of a butterfly as Mr. Mac and Peter remembered the loneliness of the dark. Peter stopped rocking. "Where do you think they went?"

"Somewhere very beautiful, Peter, where there isn't any pain. A place where they can see and walk and run."

"You mean Mishka sees again?"

"She sees you every minute of every day. I think you could see her, too."

"How, Mr. Mac, how? I'll do anything. Tell me."

"Close your eyes, Peter, as tightly as you can. Are you ready?"

"Mr. Mac, are you coming with me?"

"Yes, Peter, I'm right beside you."

"Then, I'm ready."

"Now, let's pretend you're going on a wonderful journey—
beyond the sun, beyond the moon, and beyond the stars."

Peter felt himself lifted heavenward. He felt the magic and the joy and the wonder of seeing what he had loved and lost returned to him. The broken pieces of his heart moved back together as if brushed by the wings of angels.

"I see her, Mr. Mac, I see her," Peter's voice trembled. "She's running! She's smiling. I could always tell when she was smiling."

"I see her, too, Peter. They're friends. They're going to take good care of each other."

Peter opened his eyes. "Mr. Mac, will Mishka remember me?"

"Peter, even if you become a bent old man with white hair and lines on your face, Mishka will know you as her beautiful, kind, brown-eyed boy."

"So, they never forget?" Peter yearned for a promise.

"They never forget, my friend."

Peter stood up and stretched his legs. "Um, Mr. Mac, I don't really hate ice cream."

"Then, Peter, when you come back, we'll have some together. That old chair liked your company."

Peter started down the porch steps, then suddenly turned around. "Mr. Mac, your friend—it was Mrs. MacIntyre, right?"

"Yes, Peter, she was the best friend I ever had."

The End